Brielle ☺
Chris Brunel.

MW00904615

To Lucia Mei
From Maria &
Bryan

The Owl
and the Orchestra

Photo Credits:
Michael Ensminger, www.michaelensminger.com
Lauren di Scipio, www.laurendiscipio.com
Jan Folsom, janfolsom@mac.com
Colorado Music Festival, www.comusic.org

They lived high above Boulder on the mountain called Flagstaff.
There were six of them. A father owl, a mother owl and four baby
owls. They lived atop of one of the tallest trees. From their home
they could watch the sun come up over the city of Boulder and
watch each morning as the city slowly came to life.

Father Owl was a big strong owl with mighty wings and a handsome beak. Mother Owl, too, had mighty wings and a handsome beak, but a soft expression that came from nurturing the baby owls. Although Father Owl was proud of his family, every now and again he felt that something was missing. He wanted some excitement but wasn't sure what it was. Then one summer evening, quite by accident, something happened that would forever change his life.

After dinner as he was flying from his perch high up on Flagstaff Mountain, he let the gentle evening breezes carry him down into Chautauqua Park, a park at the bottom of the mountain.

While circling lazily in the sky above the auditorium that was located in the park, he saw a small bird that he thought would make a good meal for the baby owls. He swooped down to catch it only to see it disappear through a hole in the wall of the auditorium.

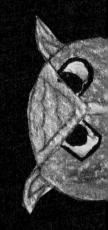

He followed the small bird into the auditorium and landed on a beam in order to see where the small bird had taken refuge. But as soon as he had settled down on the beam he became distracted by what was going on below him in the auditorium.

He saw people entering from outside and taking their places on chairs that were facing a platform that was brightly lit. The men sitting there were dressed in white shirts and dark pants, and the women wore white blouses and dark skirts, all holding strange looking objects. As he was trying to figure out what those objects were, the lights in the hall were extinguished and the lighting on the platform became even brighter.

All the people sat very quietly and soon a man in a white coat holding a slender stick strode out. The people in the auditorium began clapping and the man in the white coat bowed to them. When the clapping stopped, the man turned and facing the people on the brightly lit platform began waving his stick.

In response the people on the platform picked up the objects they had been quietly holding and began doing all manner of strange things with them.

One of the people took a stick in each hand and began beating on a round object creating a sound that reminded the owl of the thunder that he heard from his high perch on Flagstaff during summer thunder showers.

Another person picked up a large gold coiled
tube, put it to his lips and began blowing
through it, creating a sound that
reminded the owl of the sound made by
cars when they passed one another on
the road going up Flagstaff Mountain.

Another picked up a long slender silver object and produced sounds that reminded him of the sound the birds on the mountain made when they first awakened in the morning. From his perch he could not clearly see all of the various implements that were being held by the people on the platform.

He could, however, see that a number of people on the
platform had long sticks that they seemed to draw across
a piece of wood they held in their hands, although he was
unable to distinguish the sound they were making from the
sounds of the other things that he saw.

Hoping to get a better view, Father Owl flew from the rafter on which he was sitting to a rafter more directly over the platform. As he did so, he noticed that the people sitting in the darkened auditorium raised their arms and pointed towards him.

Hoping to get an even better view of the platform, he flew to yet another perch, and as he looked down, he saw that the people below continued pointing at him and following his flight.

From his perch he watched a while longer and suddenly,

for no apparent reason, the man on the stage

quit waving his arms.

At that moment thunderous applause broke out and Father Owl realized that the people were applauding for him and for the grace with which he flew from one rafter to another. Proud beyond words, his chest puffed up with pride, he flew from rafter to rafter with as much grace as he could muster and the applause continued for many minutes. When the applause finally died down the people got up and walked out of the auditorium.

When the last person had left, Father Owl quietly flew out the door
and returned to his home on Flagstaff where Mother Owl and the
baby owls were fast asleep. Father Owl fell asleep and all night
long he dreamed of his performance in Chautauqua Auditorium.

The next morning as Father Owl, Mother Owl and baby owls were having breakfast, Father Owl told the family of the adventure he had and of the thunderous applause that had greeted his performance in the auditorium. After hearing Father Owl's tale of the events of the night before, the entire owl family was terribly proud of Father Owl.

Even Father Owl, although he tried hard not to show it.

The End

CPSIA information can be obtained
at www.ICGtesting.com
Printed in the USA
LVOW05*0012070616

491460LV00008B/13/P